Chicken Licken

Written by Gill Munton

Illustrated by Christine Pym

OXFORD
UNIVERSITY PRESS

Tock!

Ow!
The sun fell
on me!

Chicken Licken ran to the barn.

Hen Len!
The sun fell on me!
Shall we go and
tell Cock Lock?

Chicken Licken and Hen Len
ran to the farmyard.

Cock Lock!
The sun fell on me!
Shall we go and
tell Duck Luck?

They all ran back to the garden.

Duck Luck!
The sun fell on me!

The sun,
Chicken Licken?

Look up,
Chicken Licken!

Can you see the nuts?
A nut fell on you!
Not the sun!

A nut?

A nut,
Chicken Licken!

The end.